Magic Ballerina
The Magic Dance

Welcome to the world of Enchantial

I have always loved to dance. The captivating music
and wonderful stories of ballet are so inspiring. So
come with me and let's follow Holly on her magical
adventures in Enchantia, where the stories of
dance will take you on a very special journey.

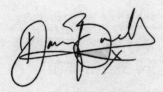

D0234332

Special thanks to
Linda Chapman and
Katie May

First published in Great Britain by HarperCollins *Children's Books* 2010
HarperCollins *Children's Books* is a division of HarperCollins *Publishers* Ltd,
77-85 Fulham Palace Road, Hammersmith, London W6 8JB

The HarperCollins website address is
www.harpercollins.co.uk

1

Text copyright © HarperCollins *Children's Books* 2010
Illustrations by Katie May
Illustrations copyright © HarperCollins *Children's Books* 2010

MAGIC BALLERINA™ and the 'Magic Ballerina' logo are
trademarks of HarperCollins Publishers Ltd.

ISBN-13 978 0 9562877 0 0

Printed and bound in England by
Clays Ltd, St Ives plc

This book has been specially written and published for World Book Day 2010.
World Book Day is a worldwide celebration of books and reading, with events held last
year in countries part as far apart as Afghanistan and Australia, Nigeria and Uruguay.
For further information please see www.worldbookday.com
World Book Day in the UK and Ireland is made possible by generous sponsorship from
National Book Tokens, participating publishers, authors and booksellers. Booksellers who
accept the £1 World Book Day Token kindly agree to bear the full cost of redeeming it.

Magic Ballerina™
The Magic Dance

Darcey Bussell

HarperCollins *Children's Books*

To Phoebe and Zoe, as they are the inspiration behind Magic Ballerina.

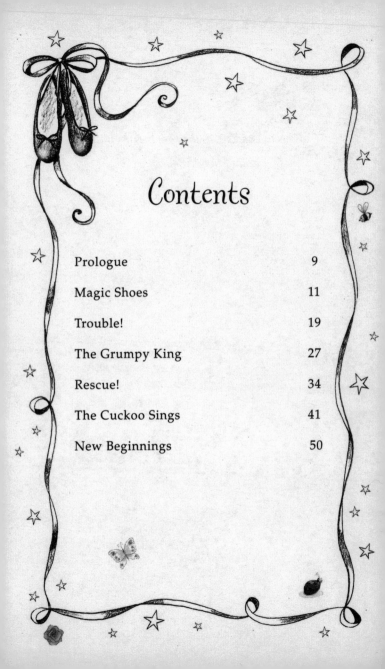

Contents

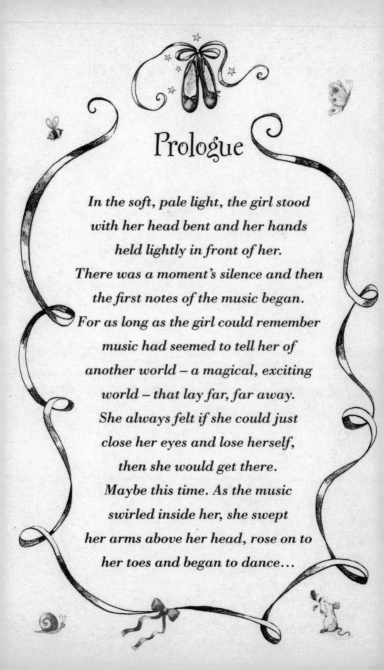

Prologue

*In the soft, pale light, the girl stood
with her head bent and her hands
held lightly in front of her.
There was a moment's silence and then
the first notes of the music began.
For as long as the girl could remember
music had seemed to tell her of
another world – a magical, exciting
world – that lay far, far away.
She always felt if she could just
close her eyes and lose herself,
then she would get there.
Maybe this time. As the music
swirled inside her, she swept
her arms above her head, rose on to
her toes and began to dance…*

Magic Shoes

Madame Za-Za opened the lid of a box on her desk and took out a pair of red ballet shoes. "I need your help, Holly," she said.

Holly Wilde stared at the shoes. Seeing them brought back so many memories. "I gave them to Chloe," she told her old ballet teacher.

"I know, but they are too tight for her

now." Madame Za-Za gently put the shoes into Holly's hands. "Sadly, she never found out how special they were."

Holly stroked the soft leather. The red ballet shoes were very special indeed, not only had they helped Holly to dance, they were magic too! They could whisk the person wearing them away to Enchantia where all the characters from the different ballets lived.

Holly had some amazing adventures there. She wished that her friend Chloe had discovered their magic too.

"The right person is not always obvious," Madame Za-Za continued. "It must be someone who has dancing deep in their heart. Will you try and find someone else while you are here visiting your aunt, Holly?"

Holly nodded and hugged the shoes tight. "Yes," she promised. "I will."

An hour later, Holly ran to the corner shop to get some milk, her dark brown hair bouncing on her shoulders. She couldn't stop thinking about what Madame Za-Za had said. Who should be the next owner of the ballet shoes? Holly thought about Rosa and Delphie who'd had the shoes before her. They were both at the Royal Ballet School now and, like her, they loved dancing passionately. She needed to find someone similar. But none of

the girls from her old ballet class seemed
quite right. They all liked ballet of course, but
when they danced, they didn't seem to
completely *live* it.

"Stop it! Right now, both of you! You're
being very naughty!"

Holly looked round at the sound of the
loud voice. A harassed-looking granny was
pushing two young children out of a nearby
house with a blue door. They were
squabbling.

A girl, a little bit younger than Holly,
followed them into the garden. She had
straight blonde hair with clips and was
wearing black leggings and a cropped pink
top.

"It's OK, Gran. I'll look after them," the
girl smiled. "You go and have a cup of tea."

"Oh, Jade, love, that's very kind," the granny said, looking relieved. "I've got such a headache."

Holly watched curiously as the girl – Jade – turned to the younger two.

"Come on, I'll teach you some more of that dance."

They ran over to her, grinning, and she began a cool spinning, stomping street dance. Holly was impressed. She'd never learned street dance herself, but Jade was great at it. She danced as if she really loved it, looking totally lost in the moment. *Just like me when I do ballet,* Holly thought.

An idea jumped into her head. Jade clearly loved to dance, so maybe she would be a good owner for the shoes? Impulsively, Holly went over to the fence. "Hi there!"

Jade stopped. "Hi."

"I'm Holly. I was watching you dance.
You're brilliant! Do you do ballet too?"

Jade laughed. "Why would I want to do
ballet?" She made it sound as if Holly had
asked her if she liked catching spiders for a
hobby.

"Ballet's amazing," said Holly in
surprise. "You should try it."

"What? Put my hair in a bun and wear a
silly tutu? No thanks!"

Holly flushed. "You don't have to wear a
tutu, you know."

"Yeah, right," Jade looked at her
disbelievingly.

"Come on, Jade. Do some more
dancing!" the two younger girls cried.

"Yeah, proper dancing – not *ballet!*" said
Jade, turning away from Holly and starting
to dance again.

Holly marched off crossly. What a
horrible girl! To think she'd been thinking
about giving the ballet shoes to *her!*

I'll have to find someone else, she thought.

The question was… who?

Trouble!

When Holly got home, she went upstairs
and put on the red shoes. They were tight
on her feet now, but she couldn't resist
dancing in them a little bit. Stepping
forward she spun round when suddenly her
feet started to tingle. Looking down, she
saw the shoes were glittering!

"Oh, wow!" Holly gasped as a cloud of

silver sparkles surrounded her. "I must be going to Enchantia again!"

She whirled up in the air and spun around and around until she felt her feet gently meet the ground. As the sparkles cleared, she saw she was in the courtyard of the Royal Palace. Excitement fizzed through her. Why was she here? The shoes only ever brought her to Enchantia when there was a problem.

She frowned. It was a lovely spring day, but something felt wrong. There was a strange stillness in the air and the flowers all seemed caught in the moment before they bloomed. A large maypole stood in the centre of the courtyard, its ribbons trailing limply.

Suddenly a large white cat came dancing out of the castle. He was slightly taller than

Holly and wore a black hat and a gold waistcoat. "Holly!"

He ran over, leaping into the air. Landing lightly, he grabbed her hands and spun her round. "Oh, my sparkling eyes. You're back!"

Holly hugged him. "Oh, Cat. I've missed you. What's going on?" She motioned around with her hand. "Why does it all feel so strange? Like… like…"

"Like everywhere is caught just before the start of spring?"

Holly nodded.

"No one knows," the White Cat replied. "The First Cuckoo of Spring hasn't sung yet – he has to sing in this courtyard to make spring start in Enchantia. But I don't think that's why the shoes have brought you here. We have another problem. It's King Tristan. He…"

"Move, you idiots!" A voice roared from inside the palace.

"Here he comes now. Quick! It's best to keep out of his way at the moment." The White Cat whisked Holly behind the maypole just as King Tristan came stomping out, pushing two footmen out of his way as he did so.

"Where's the food I ordered?" he demanded as a flock of servants hurried after him. He pointed at each of them in turn. "I want pies and cakes, biscuits and cream buns, and I want them now – now, now, NOW!"

"Yes, Your Majesty!"

"Of course, Your Majesty!"

As the servants rushed away, King Tristan laughed gleefully. Holly was astonished. The King was usually so wise and kind. This wasn't like him at all.

The White Cat was looking anxious. "He's been like this for several days now," he explained. "No one knows why. He's locked half of the servants in the dungeon and the other half he has running around at his beck and call."

The King looked beadily at the servants. "No dancing, remember," he growled. "Anyone who dances will be locked in the dungeons!"

"No dancing?" Holly whispered in horror to the White Cat.

Queen Isabella came hurrying out. "Oh, my dear," she said, touching the King's shoulder. "Are you quite sure you're all right? Why don't you go and have a little lie down?"

"Get off me, you silly woman! Look at you! Your hair is like a nest, your dress should be in the dustbin and your nose makes you look like a horse!"

"Oh!" Queen Isabella's eyes filled with tears and, turning, she ran back to the palace. The King chortled and, pulling out a mirror, examined himself in it vainly.

Holly looked at her friend. "Whatever's the matter with him?"

"I don't know." The White Cat looked at her pleadingly. "Do you think you can help us?"

Holly gulped. "I'll try!"

The Grumpy King

As King Tristan stomped around, shouting at everyone again, Holly watched, astonished. He was behaving far more like King Rat than King Tristan! King Rat lived in a smelly castle with all his mouse guards. He hated dancing and was always thinking up ways to try and stop it. Luckily, Holly had foiled his schemes before.

"I just don't know what's wrong with the King," said the White Cat, as King Tristan started to wolf down a pie. "He's not himself at all!"

Not himself! Holly felt something click in her brain. "Maybe that's it, Cat! Maybe he's *not* himself! Perhaps he's not King Tristan at all! Maybe that's someone else disguised as him!"

The White Cat's eyes widened. "Oh, my fluffy tail! I never thought about that."

Holly's thoughts raced. "We need to get closer to have a proper look. Is there any way we can magic him asleep?"

"There is a special dance that sends people to sleep," the White Cat replied. "Rosa did it once to calm a sea serpent. I can't do it because cats can't make the magic

happen in sleeping dances. But I could show you how it goes and you could try."

Holly nodded eagerly and so as the King gobbled down the food on the table, the White Cat secretly showed Holly the soft, swaying moves of the lullaby dance.

They were just finishing when King Tristan seemed to notice the maypole.

"What's THAT still doing there?" he
demanded. "I told you to take it down.
Stupid maypole. I hate spring with all the
silly bouncy lambs and people dancing. Get
rid of it!"

The White Cat gasped. "We can't do that,"
he said to Holly. "We have to dance round
the maypole when the First Cuckoo sings to

make sure we have a long and lovely springtime."

"Do it NOW!" yelled the King.

"I can't let him do this. I've got to stop him." The White Cat dashed out. "Your Majesty, please…"

"Oh, not you again!" groaned King Tristan, rolling his eyes. "What is it this time, furball?"

"You can't take the maypole down," protested the White Cat.

"CAN'T!" King Tristan exploded. "How dare you tell me I *can't*! I've had enough of you, you overgrown kitty. Take him to the dungeons! Not to the deepest one, though," he added quickly to the guards who were reluctantly surrounding the White Cat. "Anyone who goes in there will have their tai… I mean *heads*," he cleared his throat hastily, "yes, they'll have their heads cut off!"

Holly watched in horror as her friend was pulled away, looking despairingly over his shoulder at her. Oh no, what should she do now?

There was only one thing for it. She *had* to do the dance!

I hope this works! Holly took a deep breath and moved out from behind the maypole. Keeping her arms low, she swayed dreamily on the spot, just as the White Cat had showed her.

King Tristan jumped to his feet and pointed at her. "It's you! The meddling girl with the shoes! Guards!" he yelled. "GET HER!"

Rescue!

Holly's heart pounded. *Keep on dancing*, she told herself as the guards approached. *The magic will work. It will!* She began to move in a circle, turning slow pirouettes, focusing on her steps and blocking everything else out.

The guards began to yawn and the King swayed. "I feel.... I feel…" Suddenly, his chin sank into a bowl of cream and he fell fast asleep!

I did it! Holly thought in astonishment. She looked around. Everyone in the courtyard had gone to sleep!

Heart beating, she raced over and peered under the King's wig, but he really did look like King Tristan.

It's not a disguise. It is him! Holly swallowed, feeling suddenly very foolish. Now what was she going to do?

Just then, there was a bright flash of movement and the White Cat burst into the courtyard.

"Cat!" Holly gasped.

"Yes! It's me! The guards fell asleep as we were leaving the courtyard."

"But why aren't *you* asleep?" Holly demanded.

"I told you, cats can't do sleeping dances – we can't be affected by them either. We're too lively when we dance." He proved his

point by leaping up, crossing his feet over eight times. "So *is* the King someone in disguise?"

Holly shook her head. "Not unless it's a spell or something to make them look exactly like King Tristan."

"It can't be, spells of disguise don't usually last for long and he's been like this for days now…"

The White Cat broke off and stared at Holly. "Of course! That's it!"

"What?" demanded Holly.

"The Cuckoo Spell! It's a special spell which lets you take the place of someone else, just like a cuckoo takes the place of another bird in a nest. You need tail feathers from the First Cuckoo of Spring…"

"And the First Cuckoo has disappeared!" exclaimed Holly.

"But who would do the Cuckoo Spell?" said the White Cat, his eyes wide. "And where's the real King Tristan?"

The fake King stirred. He blinked and mumbled something again about the deepest dungeon.

Holly quickly started to do the dance and after a few seconds, he went back to sleep.

"Did you hear
what he said
about the
deepest
dungeon?"
Holly
breathed. "He
didn't want
anyone to go there

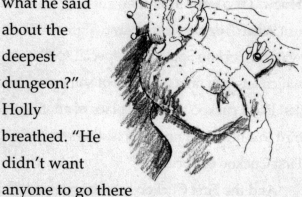

before." Her eyes met the White Cat's and
saw the same realisation dawning there.
"Do you think… maybe…?"

"Let's go and see!" cried the White Cat.

Holly and the White Cat raced to the
dungeons, heading for the very deepest one.
As they pulled the bolts back, there was a

loud squawk and a fed-up looking cuckoo
with quite a few tail feathers missing burst
out, scattering a trail of golden glitter in its
wake.

"It's the First Cuckoo!" said the White Cat.

"Cuckoo! Cuckoo!" the bird cried in delight.

"Cat! Holly!" King Tristan came charging
out following the cuckoo. "You rescued me!"

"But who imprisoned you, Your Majesty?"
asked the White Cat.

King Tristan was already striding away.

"Who do you think? Just wait till I get my hands on him!"

Holly grabbed her friend's paw. "Come on! Let's follow!"

The Cuckoo Sings

Holly and the White Cat ran out into the courtyard behind the King. The First Cuckoo was singing loudly. The buds on the cherry trees had already burst open, a light breeze caught the ribbons of the maypole and the daffodils in the flowerbeds bloomed. The guards were starting to wake up and look round in astonishment.

"Oh, my glimmering whiskers!" cried the White Cat, pointing. "The Cuckoo Spell is broken too – look!"

Holly stared in astonishment as the fake King grew black greasy fur and his cloak turned red. Then his face transformed into a pointed snout and his eyes became beady.

"It IS King Rat!" gasped Holly.

"King Rat!" bellowed King Tristan who was just ahead of them.

The rodent sat up groggily. "What's going on?" He looked down at himself. "What…?" As he saw King Tristan striding towards him, his eyes snapped fully open and he jumped to his feet. "OK, now… hang on, Tristan. No need for hard feelings is there! Just my idea of a little joke." The evil rat backed away as King Tristan advanced with his sword drawn. "Haven't you got a sense of… WAAAAA!" With a yell, he tripped over the edge of a flowerbed and landed on his back in the middle of the yellow daffodils. As he sat up, a particularly large daffodil landed upside down on his head.

King Tristan stopped, his roars of anger turning to guffaws as everyone joined in with the laughter.

King Rat scrambled to his feet.

"Guards!" shouted King Tristan through his laughter. "Take him away! He can see how he likes it in the dungeons for the next twenty-four hours while we celebrate spring!"

"What? You're going to be *dancing*?" King Rat looked at them all in horror and then pulling away from the guards, he ran into

the palace, his cloak flapping. "Let me into the dungeons, RIGHT NOW!"

Holly laughed and the White Cat swung her round. "You did it! You did it Holly! You saved the day!"

The Queen ran out and hugged the King just as the musicians started to play. The spring celebrations had begun!

They danced around the maypole until they were too tired to dance any more and then had a feast of all the food that King Rat hadn't eaten.

"Oh, Cat," said Holly looking round at the bustling courtyard. "I can't bear not to come to Enchantia again, but I must pass the shoes on."

Magic Ballerina

"You'll come back," the White Cat told her.
"Even without the shoes, the magic will bring
you. It always does."

Holly felt a rush of relief.

"Just make sure you give those shoes to
someone who has dancing deep in their
heart," the White Cat reminded her.
"Remember, it's what's deep down that
matters, Holly."

Holly felt her feet start to tingle. The shoes were glowing! "Oh, goodness! I'm going home! Bye, Cat!"

"Goodbye!" cried the White Cat, hugging her.

And in a sparkling haze of colour, Holly was swept away.

New Beginnings

Holly was set back down in her bedroom.
It was always strange coming back because
no time had ever passed while she was
away. Holly thought about everything that
had happened.

"It's what's deep down that matters," she
whispered, knowing it was true. King Rat
might have looked like King Tristan, but

underneath the surface he had been his usual horrid self. And it could work the other way round too. Holly remembered the first time she'd visited Enchantia. She'd been prickly and unfriendly, but the White Cat had seen beyond the surface and become her friend. She was very glad he had.

Holly stood up. She knew what she had to do.

✦ ☆ ✦ ☆ ✦ ☆ ✦

Ten minutes later, Holly stopped at a house with a blue door. There was no one in the garden. She ran up to the letterbox with a package in her hands. She had written a note on it:

Dear Jade,

These shoes are for you. I know you love dancing and I really hope you find out how special they are. Madame Za-Za's ballet school is just down the road and she is a brilliant teacher. Go and see her – and take the shoes. You won't regret it. I promise.

She hadn't signed it.

Hearing a noise, she quickly pushed the package through the letterbox and then turned and ran.

She hurried down the street feeling light inside. She'd done what Madame Za-Za had asked and though she might not have the shoes any more, the White Cat's words were ringing in her ears: *You'll come back.*

I will, Holly thought happily. A cloud of cherry blossom drifted down. She laughed and pirouetted around, the pink flowers settling in her dark hair.

Meet other girls in Enchantia over the page…

Hello, I'm Delphie. I wasn't sure why Madame Za-Za gave me a dusty pair of red ballet shoes until they started to glow and whisked me away to Enchantia! Sugar (also known as the Sugar Plum Fairy) befriended me there and we've had lots of magic times trying to outwit King Rat and spoil his evil plans. Together we've saved enchanted guests at a masked ball, broken wicked spells and ensured the Queen's birthday show was perfect!

Hair colour: Brown

Eye colour: Blue

Likes: practising ballet excercises, Enchantia

Dislikes: King Rat

Favourite ballet: The Nutcracker

Best friend in Enchantia: Sugar

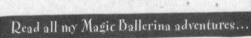

Read all my Magic Ballerina adventures...

Hi, I'm Rosa. I've always loved dancing! Madame
Za-Za tells me to slow down and concentrate on
what I'm doing, but dancing is just so exciting.
Delphie gave me the precious red ballet shoes and,
before I knew it, I was in Enchantia meeting all the
ballet characters. Nutmeg (Sugar's sister) and I
have been on lots of adventures: rescuing an
enchanted princess, finding stolen treasure and
thwarting the Wicked Fairy at every turn.

Hair colour: Blonde

Eye colour: Blue

Likes: Olivia my best friend, making my mum happy

Dislikes: Making mistakes or losing my temper

Favourite ballet: Swan Lake

Best friend in Enchantia: Nutmeg

Read all my Magic Ballerina adventures...

7 Magic Ballerina — Rosa and the Secret Princess — Darcey Bussell

8 Magic Ballerina — Rosa and the Golden Bird — Darcey Bussell

9 Magic Ballerina — Rosa and the Magic Moonstone — Darcey Bussell

10 Magic Ballerina — Rosa and the Special Prize — Darcey Bussell

11 Magic Ballerina — Rosa and the Magic Dream — Darcey Bussell

12 Magic Ballerina — Rosa and the Three Wishes — Darcey Bussell

Hi, my name's Holly and I love ballet more than anything. Dancing makes me think of my mum because she's a professional dancer. I love the emotions and stories in ballet, sometimes I get so carried away I forget where I am! Luckily I'm always in the best places: dancing at Madame Za-Za's or in Enchantia! The White Cat and I have done so much there: protecting Cinderella from an evil magician, reuniting Beauty and the Beast, and even making things right in the Land of Sweets!

Hair colour: Dark brown

Eye colour: Green

Likes: Expressing myself through dancing

Dislikes: Feeling left out

Favourite ballet: Sleeping Beauty (particularly the Rose Adagio dance)

Best friend in Enchantia: The White Cat

Read all my Magic Ballerina adventures...

Hiya. I'm Jade and I think dancing is the best!
Street dance is my thing but the red ballet shoes
that arrived in that mysterious package have
made me curious. Maybe I will go see what's
going on at Madame Za-Za's ballet school...

Hair colour: Blonde

Eye colour: Brown

Likes: Street dance, dressing up

Dislikes: Rules – boring!

Favourite ballet: I don't know yet…

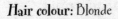

Read my Magic Ballerina adventures coming soon!

STAGECOACH
THEATRE ARTS SCHOOLS
WWW.STAGECOACH.CO.UK

Love to perform? Dream of the stage?
WIN a scholarship to a Stagecoach performing arts school!

To celebrate World Book Day, we've teamed up with Stagecoach theatre schools to offer one lucky winner the chance of a lifetime with a free one year scholarship to a Stagecoach school of their choice. Learn to sing, dance and act in a fun and friendly environment!

For your chance to win, and for more details visit www.magicballerina.com

5 runners up will win a complete set of 20 Magic Ballerina books!

Buy more great Magic Ballerina books direct from
HarperCollins at 10% off recommended retail price.
FREE postage and packing in the UK.

Delphie and the Magic Ballet Shoes	ISBN 978 0 00 728607 2
Delphie and the Magic Spell	ISBN 978 0 00 728608 9
Delphie and the Masked Ball	ISBN 978 0 00 728610 2
Delphie and the Glass Slippers	ISBN 978 0 00 728617 1
Delphie and the Fairy Godmother	ISBN 978 0 00 728611 9
Delphie and the Birthday Show	ISBN 978 0 00 728612 6
Rosa and the Secret Princess	ISBN 978 0 00 730029 7
Rosa and the Golden Bird	ISBN 978 0 00 730030 3
Rosa and the Magic Moonstone	ISBN 978 0 00 730031 0
Rosa and the Special Prize	ISBN 978 0 00 730032 7
Rosa and the Magic Dream	ISBN 978 0 00 730033 4
Rosa and the Three Wishes	ISBN 978 0 00 730034 1

All priced at £3.99

To purchase by Visa/Mastercard/Maestro simply call
08707871724 or fax on **08707871725**

Magic Ballerina
Darcey Bussell

Buy more great Magic Ballerina books direct from
HarperCollins at 10% off recommended retail price.
FREE postage and packing in the UK.

Holly and the Dancing Cat   ISBN   978 0 00 732319 7

Holly and the Silver Unicorn   ISBN   978 0 00 732320 3

Holly and the Magic Tiara   ISBN   978 0 00 732321 0

Holly and the Rose Garden   ISBN   978 0 00 732322 7

Holly and the Ice Palace   ISBN   978 0 00 732323 4

Holly and the Land of Sweets   ISBN   978 0 00 732324 1

Coming Soon:

Jade and the Enchanted Wood   ISBN   978 0 00 734875 6

Jade and the Surprise Party   ISBN   978 0 00 734876 3

Jade and the Silver Flute   ISBN   978 0 00 734877 0

Jade and the Carnival   ISBN   978 0 00 734878 7

All priced at £3.99

To purchase by Visa/Mastercard/Maestro simply call
08707871724 or fax on 08707871725

To pay by cheque, send a copy of this form with a cheque made payable to
'HarperCollins Publishers' to: Mail Order Dept. (Ref: BOB4),
HarperCollins Publishers, Westerhill Road, Bishopbriggs, G64 2QT,
making sure to include your full name, postal address and phone number.

From time to time HarperCollins may wish to use your personal data
to send you details of other HarperCollins publications and offers.
If you wish to receive information on other HarperCollins publications
and offers please tick this box ☐

Do not send cash or currency. Prices correct at time of press.
Prices and availability are subject to change without notice.
Delivery overseas and to Ireland incurs a £2 per book postage and packing charge.

Look out for Anna Wilson's new website –

it's full of barking mad and purr-fectly fun chaos!

Read cool stories

Send us your cutest pet pics for our gallery

Find out if you're destined for dogs or craving a cat

Oh no! There'll be dogs on this website too!

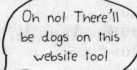

WIN amazing prizes!

And loads more cat-astrophic stuff!

www.panmacmillan.com/annawilson

Kittens always have
the last word . . .

Kitten
Smitten

by Anna Wilson

Read more about Jaffa and Bertie
in the purr-fectly zany KITTEN
SMITTEN, out now!

Does Summer ever get her own
puppy? Find out the full story in the
hilariously barking mad

Puppy Love

by Anna Wilson

Out now!

Kitten Chaos

This book has been specifically written and published for World Book Day 2010. World Book Day is a worldwide celebration of books and reading, with events held last year in countries as far apart as Afghanistan and Australia, Nigeria and Uruguay. For further information please see *www.worldbookday.com*

World Book Day in the UK and Ireland is made possible by generous sponsorship from National Book Tokens, participating publishers, authors and booksellers. Booksellers who accept the £1 World Book Day Token kindly agree to bear the full cost of redeeming it.

·Anna Wilson·

Kitten chaos

Illustrated by MOIRA MUNRO

MACMILLAN CHILDREN'S BOOKS

First published 2010 by Macmillan Children's Books
a division of Macmillan Publishers Limited
20 New Wharf Road, London N1 9RR
Basingstoke and Oxford
Associated companies throughout the world
www.panmacmillan.com

ISBN 978-0-956-28771-7

1 3 5 7 9 8 6 4 2

A CIP catalogue record for this book is available from
the British Library.

Printed and bound in the UK by CPI Mackays, Chatham ME5 8TD

Life with my gorgeous
kitten Jaffa had become
complicated. She had changed
overnight from a cute, cuddly,
playful little thing into a furry
bundle of nerves. It had started with
her leaving a ton of dead mice in
some pretty awkward places (the
microwave, on top of the telly, Dad's
laptop case . . .) and now she'd
decided that she was too scared to
go outside. Dad was *not* impressed,
as on top of all the mess this meant
clearing out a litter tray every day.
But I was worried. When I asked Jaffa
what was going on, she refused to
tell me anything. (NO, I'm not crazy
– I *can* talk to cats.) I was getting to

the end of my tether when Dad gave
me the welcome news that my old
friend Kaboodle was coming to stay
for a few days. Maybe he, a fellow cat,
would be able to get to the bottom of
my kitten's strange behaviour . . .

🐾 🐾 🐾

Kaboodle and I were having a
chat in my room while Dad
worked in his study. I was
telling the
little black
and white cat
all about Jaffa's
bizarre new
phobia.

6

'Something must have really
spooked her. The mice and the mess
she's been making are one thing, but
now with this freaky attitude she
has about the Big Outside . . . Dad's
threatened to find her a new home.'

'Oh, he will *not*!' Kaboodle hissed.
'It's a good job I'll be around for a
few days . . .'

'That reminds me, how on earth
did Ms Pinkington twist Dad's arm
into letting you stay?' I asked. Ms
P, otherwise known as Fenella, was
Kaboodle's owner. She was an actor
and had once been our neighbour.
'Like I said, he was on the verge of
chucking Jaffa out, and then you and
Ms P turn up and suddenly cats are

flavour of the month again.'

'Oh, you know, Ms P is busy with a new play which just happens to be rehearsing in the area, and all she has to do is start talking about "the stage" and your father is putty in her hands,' he purred. 'So, where is Jaffa? She hasn't said hello yet.'

'Jaffsie – Kaboodle's here!' I called.

There was a scuffling from under my wardrobe, then silence.

Kaboodle hissed softly. 'Oh, for goodness' sake come out of there.'

A tiny orange and white face peeked out.

'Hello,' Jaffa said in a small voice.

'At last,' Kaboodle sniffed. 'I thought you had been brought up with better manners, young lady.'

Jaffa lowered her eyes. 'Me is sorry, Uncle Kaboodle, but me is being so generally frighted all of the time these days.'

'Hmm, so I've been hearing. Listen, let's you and I go downstairs and you can tell me all about it,' he said. 'Coming?'

Jaffa nodded and trotted out on to the landing after Kaboodle.

'Hey!' I rushed to keep up. 'What about me?'

'I think you'll find your father would have something to say if he found you in deep debate with two cats,' Kaboodle commented archly, dancing nimbly down the stairs.

'Yeah, but I could—'

'Talking to yourself again!' Dad said, bouncing out of his room like a chirpy sparrow. 'Boy, it was good to see Fenella. She's got me all inspired to write a new play for her. I've been scribbling away like a demon since she left!'

He bounded back into his room to rattle away at his keyboard again, humming to himself like a demented wasp.

I shook my head, bemused, as I

followed the two cats downstairs. At
least he seemed to have forgotten
about his earlier threats to get rid of
Jaffa. I felt myself relax.

It was a feeling that was rather
short-lived.

KER-PLUNK!

Kaboodle sped past me to the
utility room as fast as a cheetah in the
Big Cat Olympics.

WHOOSH! BANG!

'Eeeeek!' Jaffa shrieked and shot
under a cupboard.

There was now a huge commotion
coming from the utility room. I
whizzed in: the room was empty, but
the cat flap was banging open and
shut, and there was the sound of a

serious scrap going on outside.

I peered through the glass at the
top of the door and glimpsed a
blur of black and white fur tangled
together with streaks of light brown
and orange. Suddenly the furry
tornado crashed in through the cat
flap, mewling and scratching and
completely oblivious to me.

'Kaboodle!' I cried.

A small black and white face, nose-
splodge and all, emerged from the
ball of fluff and said sourly, 'Can't
you see my paws are rather full at the
moment?'

'Yeah, mate,' said another deeper
voice. 'Leave us boys to sort things
out.'

I leaped back in surprise, then pulling myself together I said firmly, '*Excuse* me. Have we met?'

'This, it turns out, is *Bob*,' Kaboodle said, still managing to sound disdainful through a mouthful of fur. 'Say hello to Bertie, *Bob*,' he commanded.

'Grrr!' said Bob.

'Bob and I are having a small disagreement over the extremely delicate matter of territory,' Kaboodle mumbled.

Bob took advantage of the fact that Kaboodle had bitten off more than he could chew and gave him a vigorous thwack in the tummy.

'Yeoooooowl!' Kaboodle was sent flying against the washing machine.

Kitten Chaos

Bob's tail was poker straight. 'That'll
teach yer,' he snarled. Then, helping
himself to some food from Jaffa's
bowl, he zipped back through the cat
flap and was gone.

I waited while
Kaboodle gingerly
tended his wounds,
licking his paws carefully
and wincing as he washed
behind a torn ear.

'So?' I asked once he'd finished.

'So *what*?' he said tetchily.

'So what was Bob doing in my house?'

'Now who's getting all territorial?' Kaboodle crowed. 'I was doing you a favour, actually. I would have thought even *your* extremely slow human brain could work out that Jaffa needed defending from that brute Bob? Now, much as I'd love to stay and chat, I have work to do,' he snapped.

But I was too quick for him and swooped him up. He struggled, but I held his paws tight. 'Oh no you don't,' I said. 'I'm not letting you face that bully alone.'

Kaboodle wriggled irritably, but I held on. 'Oh, all right!' he said eventually. 'But put me down, please. You're squashing me.'

I reluctantly set him down and stood over him.

'Jaffa,' Kaboodle said, ignoring me altogether. 'Was that, or was that not, the beast who has been terrorizing you?'

A worried frown creased Jaffa's fluffy forehead. 'Yes, that the Big Bad Mr Bob Cat who is nasty to Jaffa.'

Kaboodle washed a paw thoughtfully. 'So, Bob has been crashing in uninvited and helping himself to *your* food?'

'Yes, Uncle Kaboodle. And he very fierce and shouty at me. If I says he can't have food, Bob go all snarly and do horrid nasty messes. Then I is getting all the trouble!' She shot me a particularly hurt look.

'I – I'm sorry we blamed you, Jaffa,' I whispered.

'I should think so too,' Kaboodle admonished. 'But there's no time for regret. If it's OK with you, Bertie, I'm going to gather some information from my contacts in the neighbourhood. I want to put together a picture of this Bob character's day-to-day movements; find out more about him.'

That did sound sensible. After

all, there couldn't be much harm in
letting Kaboodle have a chat with his
old friends.

Could there?

I tried calling my best mate Jazz that
afternoon to tell her about the weird
goings-on. We always told each other
everything. But her mum said she was
rehearsing for her dance show and
wouldn't be back until late.

'I'll get her to call you in the
morning,' she promised.

I went to bed feeling like a
spare part. The two cats had made
themselves comfy downstairs, curled

up together on the sofa, a furry yin and yang, and Dad was typing so furiously that he hadn't even stopped to eat supper with me. I tossed and turned and then drifted into a restless sleep, falling helter-skelter into a dream where I was backed into the corner of my bed with one of those old-fashioned steam trains chuntering towards me. I was desperately flattening myself against the wall to stay out of its way, but the whirring noise of the engine was getting closer and closer and my head was feeling hot and squashed and –

I jolted awake in panic to find something warm and soft pressing down on my face. I flailed at it wildly

and tried to scream, but my mouth
was full of . . . fur?

'What—?' I sat up in alarm and
the thing shot off me and landed on
the duvet with a soft thump. I warily
flicked on the light to get a better
look.

Crouching fearfully on my duvet
was a kitten, small and black as soot.
Was this a trick? I scanned the room
for Jaffa or Kaboodle, willing
myself to wake up properly and
take stock of what
was going on.

Before me was a
sight which was a bit
too much to take in
at first. All over my

room, in every conceivable nook and cranny – on top of the wardrobe, on the curtain rail, on my chair – there were cats: big ones, small ones, black, white, brown and grey ones.

'KABOOOOODLE!' I screamed. I was too freaked to care if I woke Dad.

A black and white blur hurtled in and leaped up on to my bed, landing hard on my chest and knocking the wind out of me.

'Shh!' Kaboodle hissed, his eyes flashing in the dark. 'You'll frighten them.'

'Me frighten *them*?' I gasped, pushing him off me. 'What—?'

'I'd forgotten how *stressy* you can get,' Kaboodle sneered. 'I was going to

explain in the morning, but seeing as you're awake . . .'

Two white kittens who had been doing a tightrope act on the curtain rail shimmied down and landed soundlessly on my duvet. They tiptoed over to Kaboodle and touched noses and then snuggled down, top to tail, and immediately fell asleep.

'I'm listening,' I said, trying not to get distracted by the cute kittens.

Kaboodle gave his shoulder a quick lick; I coughed loudly, and he flinched.

'All right, all right,' he bristled. 'It's that ruffian.'

'Hmm?' I prompted.

Kaboodle glared at me. 'Bob. Well,

you saw what a brute he was to *me*.
You wouldn't believe what else he's
been up to!'

'It wouldn't have something to do
with the rather *cat-astrophic* state of my
bedroom?' I said, sarcasm oozing from
every word.

'Ha ha, I don't think,' he hissed,
hackles raised. 'Bob's been terrorizing
the entire neighbourhood! He's been
attacking my friends and relations,
helping himself to their meals – no
wonder poor Jaffa is frightened.'

A light went on somewhere in the
depths of my sleep-deprived brain.
'Ah! I get it: you thought you'd be the
local hero and bring all Bob's victims
round to my place for the night?'

Kaboodle glanced away shiftily.
'Erm, yes. Well, perhaps not just for
the night—'

'Oh no,' I cut in. 'They can't stay.
I'd be known as the neighbourhood
catnapper!' I shivered as I remembered
how I had felt when our new
neighbour Fiona had 'adopted' Jaffa
a few months ago. 'Can't you reason
with Bob?'

Kaboodle gave a snort of derision.
'You don't *reason* with a cat who has
a rock for a brain. These poor victims
of abuse need to stay here while I
deal with that beast. And three of the
families concerned are on holiday
anyway. By the time they come back
I'll have the situation under wraps.'

I glanced at my clock. Half past one. I could stay up all night arguing, or I could get some rest and think things through in the morning.

'Let's talk about this later,' I yawned. Then something occurred to me. 'Where's Jaffa?' I asked sharply.

'She was playing with the twins earlier.' Kaboodle gestured to the snoozing white kittens. 'They wore her out, so she's having a rest behind the curtains.' He jumped down lightly. 'You get back to sleep yourself, Bertie. I'll tell this lot to stay well hidden.' And he disappeared.

If I hadn't been so tired, I might have asked Kaboodle for a few details on how he thought he was going to

manage to keep at least twelve cats
hidden (I'd counted all the ones in
my room while he was talking). I
didn't exactly live in a mansion; there
weren't that many places you could
hide.

But I *was* tired. I lay back and
surveyed my uninvited guests. They
gazed back, lost and forlorn.

'Kaboodle told us you'd take care
of us,' a grey and white cat piped up.

Poor little things. It wasn't their
fault Kaboodle had dragged them
away from their homes.

'Bob's a bully!' squealed another
kitten.

'He ate all my food last week.'

'He bashed me on the nose!'

'He stole my treats.'

I waved my hands frantically. 'Shh, you'll wake Dad!' I hissed. He'll freak—'

'Bertie!' Dad's voice drifted across the landing. 'Bertie?'

Oh no! Footsteps . . .

The door opened a fraction; I gestured wildly to the cats to hide.

The door opened a tiny bit further just as I noticed the tabby cat sitting in the middle of my bed. I quickly shoved the duvet over him, muttering at him to stay hidden.

Dad peered in. 'You OK? Had a nightmare?'

You could say that.

'Mfffgugglgle.' A muffled squeaking

noise came from under the duvet.

'What's that?' Dad shot a suspicious glance round the room.

'Mmmffffgugulg!'

'NOTHING!' I said too loudly. 'Nothing,' I repeated a bit more normally as Dad frowned at me. 'I – er – I was just humming this new song I heard on Jazz's iPod. Mmm–mmm–merm–merm–mmmm!' I hummed like an oversized bumblebee.

'Ri-ight,' Dad said, slowly backing out as if I'd turned into a dangerous lion that was about to pounce. 'Maybe you could save the late-night entertainment for another time, eh?'

I did an over-the-top giggle as if he'd just said the most hilarious thing

in the world. 'You are too much, Dad!'

'Night then,' he said, shaking his head in puzzlement.

As soon as it was light, I leaped out of bed and made a hurried search of the room. All the cats were still snoozing in their various hiding places, so I scooted down to the kitchen to check on Jaffa and Kaboodle. Both cats were sitting on kitchen chairs, busily washing themselves after their breakfast. Dad was at the table, absent-mindedly munching a slice of toast while reading the paper.

So far so normal.

I banged pots and pans together noisily so that Dad wouldn't hear me talking to the cats.

'You two – upstairs, now!' I ordered in a low voice.

'Bertie! I'm trying to read,' Dad complained, shaking the pages irritably. 'Can't you be quiet?'

Kaboodle looked up crossly, one paw hanging in mid-air. 'Just let us finish washing, can't you?'

'NO!' I spat angrily.

'Hey! There's no need for that,' Dad protested from over the top of the paper. 'I'll go and read in the sitting room, shall I?' He scraped his chair back.

'We can tell when we're not wanted. Come along, Jaffa,' said Kaboodle sniffily.

'Yeah, and don't come back until I tell you to,' I hissed.

Dad frowned. 'Someone's got out of bed the wrong side this morning,' he muttered.

I started breaking eggs into a bowl. 'Sorry, I'm just hungry,' I said to Dad. 'I'm going to make pancakes.'

'OK. Call me when they're ready,' Dad said, turning to go into the sitting room. 'Hey!' He jumped back in alarm. 'Did you just see that?'

'What?' I whipped round.

'Two white kittens,' Dad said shakily, pointing into the hall.

'Uh-huh-ha-ha-haaa! Daaaaaad, you're hallucinating! You've been working too hard,' I blustered.

'But I could have sworn . . .' Dad muttered, going to investigate.

There was only one thing for it. I dropped the bowl.

CRASH! Egg yolk ran into puddles on the floor.

'Oh, Bertie!' Dad cried. 'Those

were the only ones left.'

'Sorrr-eeee,' I wailed, trying to act like it was an accident. 'Could we have bacon and sausages instead? Can you see if we've got any? I'll clear this lot,' I babbled. I caught sight of the grey and the tabby cats trotting past. 'Oh,' I yelled desperately, 'there are mushrooms in the fridge, aren't there?'

'You don't like mushrooms,' he said slowly.

'Me? Mushrooms? Me and mushrooms, we're like this,' I jabbered, holding up two fingers close together to show just how keen on each other mushrooms and I were. 'Yeah, I love mushrooms, me. I eat other people's

at school. Yeah, yummy, yummy mushrooms!' I sang out louder than ever as I spotted the rest of the cats running down the hall.

'Okaaaay,' Dad muttered, shooting me a you–are–so–not–behaving–normally look. He glanced in the fridge while I let out the breath I'd been holding. 'There's no mushrooms in here,' he said. 'Or bacon. I think I'll pop to the shops.'

'Oh, would you?' I put on my most pleading tone. 'I'm sooooo hungry. Toast just isn't going to do it for me after the night I've had.'

I watched Dad like a hawk as he grabbed his shoes and headed for the front door, praying that the other

kittens would have the sense to stay
hidden until he had gone.

DING-DONG!

What NOW . . . ?

'Hi, Jazz,' I heard Dad say. 'Come
in. Bertie's making a mess of breakfast.
You can go through and help her
clean up, if you like.'

'Oh, ha ha ha ha, Mr F!' Jazz's
voice tinkled. 'You are, like, soooooo
unfunny.'

I tiptoed into the hall to see some
other unwanted feline guests hovering
at the top of the stairs. I mimed at
them to stay silent, and walked up to
the door.

'Hi, Jazz!' I said breezily. 'Let's go to
yours.'

'Oh no you don't, young lady,' Dad cut in. 'You're not going anywhere until the kitchen is spotless and we've eaten some breakfast.'

Jazz grinned maddeningly. 'Yeah, I could murder a bacon butty – OW!' She swerved violently and banged her arm on the door as a streak of orange and brown shot past her, claws out, teeth bared, uttering an ear-splitting howl of indignation.

'Miiiaooow! Get off my back, can't yer?' Bob was shrieking.

'If anyone should be getting off people's backs around here, it's you!' Kaboodle screeched.

Jaffa chose that moment to appear in the hall from her latest hiding place.

She took one look at the seething, boiling mass of fur that was rolling around on the rug, squeaked and hurled herself at Dad's legs, using them as a ladder.

'Aieeee!' Dad cried, leaping from one foot to the other and batting at the little kitten, whose claws were lodged firmly in his flesh.

'Have you all gone totally INSANE?' Jazz screamed, covering her ears, her eyes as wide as a startled rabbit's.

'Kaboooooodle!' I yelled.

This is it, I thought, closing my eyes against the horror of it all and trying to concentrate on breathing. From this moment on I will no longer be

Bertie Fletcher, proud owner of Jaffa,
the lovely, cuddly orange and white
kitten. I will be catapulted back into
my former existence as petless and
unhappy Bertie: sad, lonely and utterly
miserable. Life cannot get any worse.

But of course it can, and it did, as I
saw when I opened one eye.

'What—?' Dad's jaw had dropped so
low he could have swallowed a hippo.
He was pointing a wavering finger at
something behind me and gibbering,
'Ki-ki-ki-kittens!'

Jazz too was the most shocked I
think I had ever seen her. Even more
shocked than the time someone in
our class said her dancing looked
like a rhinoceros impersonating a

chimpanzee with constipation.

'Bertie!' It was Jaffa, who'd let go of Dad and was shivering in fright. 'Save Jaffsie from the Big Bad Bob Cat!'

There was only one thing for it, and if it meant I came across as a total loony and ended my days being dragged kicking and screaming from my home by men in white coats, that was just too bad.

'Kaboodle,' I said, turning my attention fully on the little black and white cat, 'get rid of Bob and tell this lot to clear off.'

'Who's Bob?' Jazz and Dad chorused.

'Bob,' I said, praying that Jazz and Dad were already so bamboozled

they wouldn't stop and ask me why I
was talking to a bunch of cats, 'is that
bully there. He's the reason Jaffa's been
behaving so strangely recently, he's the
reason for all the messes you've been
blaming on Jaffa, and he's the reason
our house has been taken over by a
– by a posse of frightened pussies!' I
spat the words out.

Dad peered at Bob and said, 'I
recognize that cat.' He scratched
his head. 'I'd swear it's the Morrises'
moggy. But they moved away weeks
ago.'

'That's right,' said Bob gruffly. 'One
minute my family was feeding me,
giving me cuddles, letting me into
their house to let me sleep on their

beds; the next minute they were gone.'

I wave of realization crashed over me. 'So that's why you – I mean *he's* been sneaking into other people's houses to steal food.'

'Ten out of ten for observation,' Kaboodle added sarcastically.

Then Jazz came out with the strangest words I'd ever heard her say:

'The poor little kitty-cat!'

I gawped in disbelief at my friend, expecting her to break into a raucous cackle of laughter. But instead she just shook her head sadly and whispered, 'How could anyone abandon him like that? He must be so lonely.'

Her hands were clasped to her chest and she was gazing at Bob as

though he was the most beautiful
sight she had ever had the good
fortune to behold.

Dad snorted quietly, but quickly
coughed to cover it up when he too
realized
that this
was not a
laughing
matter.

For Bob
too was suddenly
looking rather
weird. His green eyes,
before so mean and steely, were
now wide and shining, and he was
staring back at Jazz with an expression
of deep devotion.

It was Kaboodle that broke the silence. 'I do believe it's a case of love at first sight,' he said.

And I had to say I agreed with him.

Anna Wilson
Puppy Love

Remember – it's not all about
the kittens! Turn over for an
exciting extract from
PUPPY LOVE
by Anna Wilson . . .

This is the story of how my wish came true. The wish that I, Summer Holly Love, have been holding close to my heart for all of my life — well, for as long as I can remember, anyway.

It's also the story of how my older sister, April Lydia Love, nearly wrecked my wish and (almost) made me wish I hadn't wished it, because of her totally weird and unforgivably embarrassing behaviour. More of that later.

Get on with the story!

Puppy Love

It began when I started YEARNING for my very oWN pUppY to have and to hold for ever and ever, Amen.

And believe me, I have prayed that a million thousand times to anyone who I thought might be listening. But for a long time it didn't seem like anyone was listening AT ALL.

Like you're not listening to me now?

The funny thing about people not listening to you, I have found, is that they only don't listen when

you're trying to tell them something
important, like how much you
are yearning for your very own
pUppY! For example, when I
used to ask Mum over and over
again she never seemed to be
listening at all, but always said,
'Hmm, maybe. Ask me again
when I'm not driving around a
roundabout/reversing into a
blinking tight car-parking space.'

But then whenever I had to tell her
things I'd rather not, like, 'I'm sorry
I seem to have got extra homework
again,' she was always on a totally
different wavelength altogether and
heard me vERY LoUd AND
CLEAR INDEED.

Puppy Love

Boy, are you long-winded.

I have to say though, I am now living proof that it really pays off to be PERSISTENT, as Molly Cook, my best friend, would say. (Molly is great at using long words and then explaining them to you so that you can just NONCHALANTLY drop them into conversations to impress people when they are not expecting it.)

So, after being persistent about the puppy for the longest time ever, I got the chance to be even more persistenter when a boy in my class

50

called Frank (who's OK most of the
time as long as you don't sit next to
him towards the end of the week
because he only
changes his
socks on a
Monday, and,
like, do they start
to honk by Wednesday afternoon)
said that his Labrador (who has the
unfortunate name of Meatball) had
had pUppIES!

At last! I
thought you'd
never get
there . . .

He brought in photos and everything.
And were those puppies CUTE or
what?

Oh stop,
this is getting
embarrassing!

Mr Elgin even let Frank stand up
in class and tell us about the puppies
being born, and how he'd stayed
up all night to watch. And then
Frank put on this kind of serious
voice you hear on the radio when
people are advertising things for sale
and said:

Every puppy needs a good home,
so if you are interested, please
do not hesitate to contact me
and arrange an appointment.

But remember, kids:
a Puppy is for Life,
Not Just for Christmas.

Which was a daft thing to say, as
we'd only just had Easter. I even still
had a stash of mini eggs left in my
secret place under my bed behind my
Celebrity Club folder, next to my
torch.

At that point Mr Elgin said, 'Thank
you, Frank, that will do. Go back to
your place, please.' So Frank did.

Puppy Love

After that I really couldn't concentrate on any lessons. I was just watching the clock on the wall, which definitely moves a lot slower than the one at home, and thinking that if I thought hard enough the hands would move faster and it would be break time quicker.

It didn't work, but at last someone rang the bell for break and we all made a beeline for the playground. I normally just go straight into the corner with Molly and we do our Celebrity Club, but today I had to have a Very Important Appointment with Frank to discuss the Puppy Situation. So that's why I made the beeline.

Frank was kicking a ball around as usual, so when I said, 'Frank, about those puppies,' he didn't hear me. Honestly, sometimes I just think I'm INVISIBLE. So I made my beeline right in front of him and did a bit of nifty footwork and got the ball off him and passed it skilfully to one of his smelly mates.

'Oi!' said Frank.

'Summer, actually,' I said, and I folded my arms like Mum does when you know she means business.

'What?' said Frank. Boys really are the thickest sandwich in the picnic basket sometimes. I tried again.

'I said, "About those puppies."'

'No, you didn't,' said Frank. 'You said, "Summer actually."'

He's right, you did

I raised my eyebrows and sighed in a particularly dramatical manner and said, 'That's my name.'

'What are you on about?' said Frank.

It was then that I knew I had to use my most Mum-like tone to get his attention. 'I want to talk to you about your puppies, Frank Gritter.'

'You'll have to make an appointment,' he said importantly and tried to get past me, back to his

football-playing mates.

'I am making an appointment right now,' I said. This is how to be truly persistent, I thought.

Frank sighed and said, 'Come round after tea – but my mum says anyone interested has to have Parental Consent.'

I wasn't sure what Parental Consent was, but I thought that it must be something to do with parents, and that I could probably get anything I wanted now that I was in such a persistent frame of mood.

'OK,' I said, and stepped to one side so that Frank could kick a ball around again and make his socks even more

sweatier. I made a mental reminder not to stand too close to him at his house that night.

Did someone mention socky-whiff? Mmmm, my favourite!